Aa

I can ADD one and one. One kitty and one kitty equals two kitties.

Bb

I can BRUSH my dolly's hair—and she won't even cry.

I can do it
ABC

By Margo Lundell

Illustrated by Barbara Lanza

A GOLDEN BOOK • NEW YORK

Golden Books Publishing Company, Inc., New York, New York 10106

Busy, busy me. There are so many things that I can do. I will tell you what they are.

Cc

I can CARRY my stuffed animals and CLIMB the stairs.

Dd

I can DIG

a hole to China . . .

Ee

or EAT a banana.

Ff

I can FLAP my arms
like a chicken . . .

Gg

or GO away.

Hh

I can HIT with a hammer
and Mommy hardly HELPS at all.

Ii

I can watch an inchworm INCH
its way across a leaf.

Jj
I can JUMP a little,
but my sister can jump higher.

Kk

I can KISS my brother,
but my brother can't kiss me.

Ll

I can LICK ice cream
and LAUGH, too.

M m

I'm very good at MARCHING.

Nn

I can NEIGH like a horse.

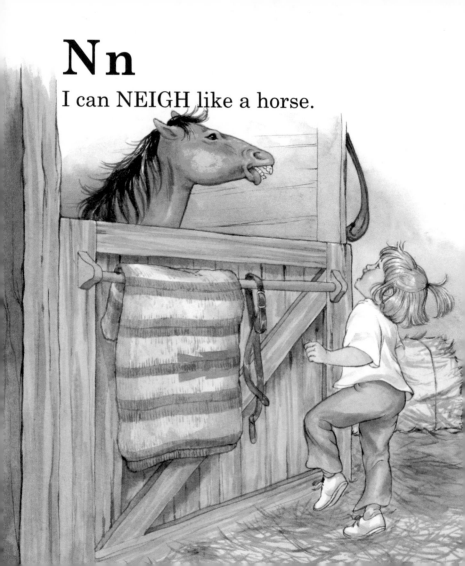

Oo

I can OPEN my mouth
and OINK like a pig.

Pp
I can PURR like a cat . . .

Q q

or QUACK like a duck.

Rr

I can REACH for the sky . . .

Ss

and SMILE because I'm happy.

Tt
I can TALK to Mommy.

Uu
I can UPSET the baby
if I wake him!

Vv

I can VACUUM for Daddy on Saturday.

Ww

I can WALK on the stones in the stream.

Xx

I can pretend I'm an airplane.
First I draw an X on the sidewalk.

Yy

Then I stand on the X
and YELL, "Watch out. Here I come!"

Z z

Then I ZOOM all the way to the end of the block.

Busy, busy me. There are so many things I can do!